Personal Space Camp

Activity and Idea Book

published by

NATIONAL CENTER for YOUTH ISSUES

A special "Thanks!" to two of the best first grade teachers in the business:
Jaime Weakend and Mary Jo Reynolds. — Julia

A Note To Educators

Personal Space is a concept that is confusing and difficult for some people (of all ages) to grasp. Everything in space needs its own space to function. The amount of personal space needed seems to be forever changing depending upon the circumstances. For a person to be at their best in any situation, they must have an adequate amount of personal space.

When students inappropriately or unknowingly invade the personal space of others, learning is often compromised. Personal space invasion is a learned behavior and can be "unlearned" through communication and practice.

This workbook is designed to offer teachers and students "hands on" activities that explore the concept of personal space. Students will gain a better understanding of what personal space is, and why it is so important.

I hope you enjoy doing these activities with your students as much as I have enjoyed creating them.

BEST!

Julia Cook

NATIONAL CENTER for YOUTH ISSUES

P.O. Box 22185 • Chattanooga, TN 37422-2185
423.899.5714 • 866.318.6294 • fax: 423.899.4547 • www.ncyi.org
ISBN: 978-1-931636-93-3 $9.95

© 2010 National Center for Youth Issues, Chattanooga, TN • All rights reserved.

Summary: A supplementary teacher's guide for *Personal Space Camp*.
Full of discussion questions and exercises to share with students.

Written by: Julia Cook • Illustrations by: Carrie Hartman
Published by National Center for Youth Issues

Printed at Starkey Printing • Chattanooga, TN, USA • August 2021

One Big Clump!

While students are out for recess, push all of their chairs and desks together in a clump in the middle of your classroom. Make it so sitting at their desks becomes next to impossible. Have them enter the room and attempt to sit in their seats. Stress the importance of how personal space is necessary to feel comfortable at school.

This activity can be repeated by having students sit any way they want to on the carpet. Some may lie down or sit very close to others. Discuss the importance of having enough personal space to do your very best.

My Personal Space Place Mat

Have students use large pieces of chart paper to draw, create and color their own personal space mat. This can be in the shape of their favorite planet, or you can let them choose their own shape. Cut out each mat and if possible, laminate it. Have students use their "Space Places" to help them define their own personal boundaries for work time. Space Place Mats give students a visual that can help them work independently and in their own space. They can be placed on the floor and serve as mats for the student to sit on or students can place their desks and chairs on top of them.

Classroom Galaxy

Materials Needed:
- Flour
- Water
- Whisk or Mixer
- Newspaper
- Scissors
- Balloons
- Paint and/or other materials
- Fishing line

Paper Mache Recipe

Pour some white flour in a bowl, and add water gradually until you have a consistency that will work well. (If available, you can use a small kitchen mixer so you don't have any lumps).

How thick should you make your paste? It's actually up to you. Experiment with thick pastes that resemble hotcake batter, and thin pastes that are runny and watery. You get to decide which one you prefer.

Keep in mind that it is the flour, and not the water, that gives strength to your paper mache sculpture. And also remember that each layer of paste and paper that is added to your project must dry completely to keep it from developing mold.

Instructions

1. Using paper mache, have your students create models of the planets in our galaxy. You may wish to divide the class into teams working on each planet as assigned.

2. Cut newspaper into strips.

3. Give each student a balloon and have them inflate it.

4. Dip strips into paper mache mixture and cover balloon. Let dry overnight. Place small needle through hardened mache and pop balloon.

5. Have students decorate the hardened mache with paint and/or other art supplies to resemble the planet assigned.

6. Hang the models to scale from the ceiling in your classroom with fishing line.

7. Explain how everything in outer space has its own space and needs that space to be the best it can be.

8. Discuss what would happen if the planets got too close together. Tangle the planets together to create the visual. Relate this example to people and the need for personal space.

Personal Space Line-Up Rope (PSLUR for short!)

Take a long, narrow piece of material (approximately 20-25 feet) or a smooth textured rope and tie multicolored pieces of material to the rope approximately 18" apart. Use square knots when tying the material to the rope so that the knots will be permanently placed and not slide up and down along the rope. Have each student grab a knot with their right hand and as a class, carry the rope through the halls. The rope will help to keep the students properly spaced while in line. Discuss what happens when kids get too close to each other in line and why it is so important to use a safe distance. You can even relate this exercise to driving, i.e. when cars follow too closely and can't stop on time.

Imaginary PSLUR!

After using the real PSLUR a few times, have students line up in a straight line and place their palms on the shoulders of the person in front of them. Have them space apart so that everyone's arms are straight. Tell them to drop their arms to their sides. This is how far apart you need to be when you are in a line. Have them reach out to grab the imaginary PSLUR knot and carry it through the hall with them.

How Much Personal Space Do I Take Up?

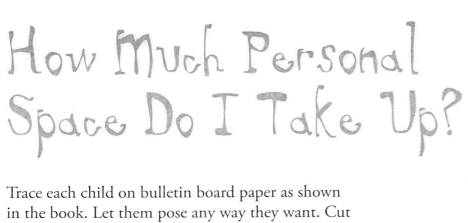

Trace each child on bulletin board paper as shown in the book. Let them pose any way they want. Cut out the shapes and laminate them if possible. Have each child hold their paper shape and practice standing with it, sitting with it, and laying it down on the carpet to show them how much space they actually take up. After this lesson, use the shapes to decorate the walls of your classroom.

Space Freeze

Play music and have students move and dance around. When the music stops, have the students freeze. They may be in their own personal space or they may be invading the personal space of another person. Have students discuss how they felt when others were invading their personal space.

Think About It

Somebody invaded MY Personal Space!

1. Explain in detail a time when somebody invaded your Personal Space and it made YOU cranky.

2. How did this make you feel?

3. What did you think of the person who invaded your space?

4. Was your situation dangerous? Why or why not?

5. Could the person who invaded your space have handled the situation differently? If so, what could he or she have done?

6. In your opinion, should the person have invaded your Personal Space? Why or why not?

Think About It... Too!

I invaded someone's Personal Space!

1. Explain in detail a time when you invaded someone's Personal Space and it made them _cranky_.

2. Why did you do it?

3. How did you feel right after you did it?

4. Knowing what you know about Personal Space, would you have handled this situation the same way? Why or why not?

5. What advice would you give to someone who is having problems with Personal Space?

Design a
Personal Space Camp T-Shirt

Directions:

Use your creativity to design a T-shirt! Make up your own logo or
slogan that will teach others how to respect personal space.

Personal Space Camp Invaders

You are a Personal Space Invader! It is your job to find examples of personal space with objects in our galaxy and invade them to figure out how they work.

Teachers:
 Take a walk around your school and playground with your students and demonstrate how things in life need their own space to work.

Have students make a list of everything they see that requires personal space to function. The concept of personal space is everywhere!!!!

Examples:

See-Saws

Swings

Books in the library

Instruments in the music room

Desks in the classroom

Food on the lunch room trays

Cars in the parking lot

Teachers' mail boxes

Bonus Project!
Have each child pick their favorite example of personal space from their list and write about it or draw a picture of it to share with the rest of the class. What could happen if personal space didn't exist for the object that they chose?

Personal Space Popcorn

Show students a small container full of un-popped popcorn. Using an air popper, pop the corn and make note of how it changes and grows. Try to fit the popped corn back into the small container. Place the popped corn into a larger container that will hold all of it.

Explain to students that as we grow and change, the amount of personal space that we need also grows and changes.

Make more popcorn and enjoy this healthy treat! Place a napkin in the center of each desk. Place ½ cup of popped corn on top of each napkin. Explain that every child has their own treat and each treat has its own space.

Ask them: "What would have happened if we had put all of the popcorn in a bowl and had everyone reach into the bowl at the same time?"

Personal Space Show and Tell

Dear Parents –

We have been learning a lot about personal space. Everything in life needs it own space to work and Personal Space examples are all around us! Please help your child find something at home that demonstrates personal space and have them bring it to school for Show and Tell. Examples might include:

- Egg carton
- Plastic baggie
- Plastic refrigerator container
- Tackle or tool box

My Very Own Personal Space!

Write about a place that you like to go all by yourself.
- What does your special place look like?
- What do you like to do when you are in your special place?
- How would you feel if someone entered your special place without your permission?

In the box below, draw a picture of your special place with you in it doing what you love to do!

_____

_____

_____

_____

_____

_____

_____

_____

_____

_____

_____

_____

Personal Space Soup Can

It is *your* job to design the label for
Personal Space Soup!

Directions:

Bring a can of food to school. Write what is in the can in marker on the bottom end. Remove the label. Cut out white paper so that it will wrap neatly around your can. Design your label. Cover your can and display. When your class project is over, donate the canned food to your local food bank.

Extra Fun!
Have the children write and perform their own commercial for their soup.

Scientific Proof

Every living thing needs its own space to grow.

We can't grow to become the best we can be if we don't have enough personal space.

Materials Needed:
Small styrofoam, plastic or paper cups
Soil
Seeds (carrot, radish, flower etc.)

Have each child fill two cups half way full of soil. In one cup, have the child plant two seeds with space in between each. In the other cup have them dig a small hole and plant 10 seeds all together.

Water every other day or as needed so that soil stays moist. Make sure you don't over water.

Have students keep a daily journal on what is happening in each of their cups.

Eventually, the cup with all of the seeds will die out because there is not enough room (personal space) to sustain growth. The other cup of seeds should flourish.

Relate this experience to people and talk about how important it is to have enough personal space.

Scientific Proof— You Be the Seed!

For a creative writing extension, tell your story from the seed's perspective using the lines below. You may use a separate sheet of paper if you need more room. You can be a seed in the crowded cup, or the seed in the cup with enough room. You can even have your story be about two seed friends – one from each cup. Use your journal that you have kept to get accurate details for your story. Have fun!

_____

_____

_____

_____

_____

_____

_____

_____

_____

_____

_____

_____

_____

_____

Your View of Personal Space

When you hear the words "personal space" what picture
do you see inside of your head?

Draw a picture of what "Personal Space" looks like to you.

Too Many Fish!!

Materials Needed:
10 gummy fish per student

Glue

Scissors

- Copy the fishbowl below, allowing two per student.

- Have student glue 9 gummy fish in one fish bowl and only one gummy fish in the other

- When they are finished, discuss how uncomfortable the crowded fish must be. There is no room to swim, no room to play etc. Compare that to the fish bowl with only one fish in it. Everything in space needs the right amount of personal space. Put the fish pictures up on your bulletin board as a visual reminder.

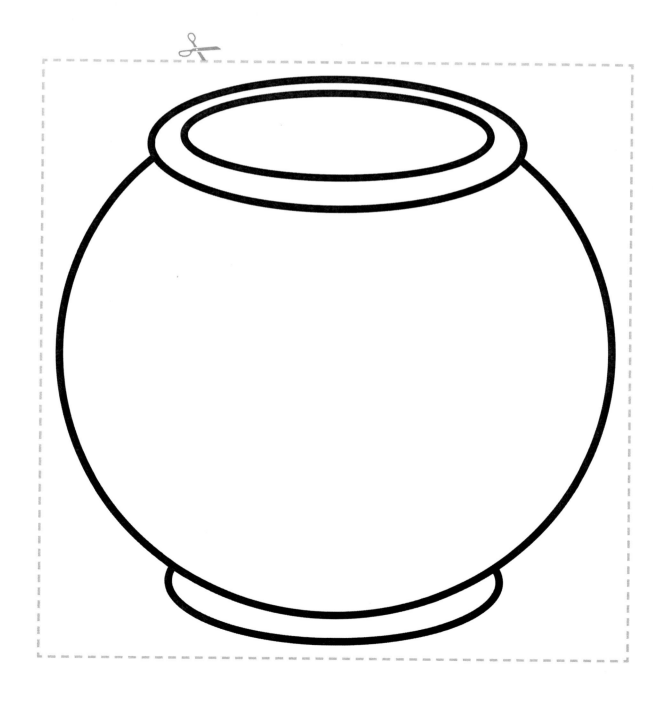

Personal Space Bubbles

Materials Needed:
Hula Hoop
Bottle of Bubbles

Instructions:

• Give each child a hula hoop and allow them to sit inside it. Explain to them that the hoops represent the edges of their personal space bubbles.

• Take out a bottle of bubbles and blow through the wand. Point out to students that personal space bubbles like regular bubbles come in all sizes.

Explain to your students that their personal space bubbles are usually about the size of the hoop they are sitting in, but sometimes their bubble is smaller – like when they are around close friends and family (Try fitting on the carpet with all of the hoops – kids will realize that their bubbles need to get smaller to fit, etc.)

Other times their personal space bubble needs to get bigger – like when they are in unfamiliar territory or around people they don't know very well, or when they are swinging on the swings outside, etc.

Personal Space Bubble Worksheet

Draw a picture of you in your personal space bubble when we are all sitting on the carpet.

Draw a picture of you in your personal space bubble when you are working at your desk.

Draw a picture of you in your personal space bubble when you are swinging on the swings out on the playground.

Draw a picture of you in your personal space bubble when a grown up you don't know tries to talk to you at the store when you are alone.

For Discussion
What do you notice about the size of your personal space bubble?
Does it always stay the same? Explain why or why not.

What Can You Make Of It?

How many words (two or more letters) can you make out of the letters found in:

PERSONAL SPACE CAMP!

Write your answers below. Use the back of the paper if you run out of room.

1. _____   13. _____

2. _____   14. _____

3. _____   15. _____

4. _____   16. _____

5. _____   17. _____

6. _____   18. _____

7. _____   19. _____

8. _____   20. _____

9. _____   21. _____

10. _____   22. _____

11. _____   23. _____

12. _____   24. _____

If the Space Shoe Fits...

Have students try to put on a pair of shoes that are too small for them and then walk around the classroom.

Even if they can get the shoes on their feet, it becomes very uncomfortable to walk in them.

Have students put on a pair of shoes that are very big for them and walk around the classroom.

The shoes may not hurt their feet, but running and jumping in them would be next to impossible.

Now, have them put their own shoes back on.

Personal space is like a pair of shoes. The size of our personal space bubble has to fit us just right and will change depending on our situation.

In order to be the best we can be, we need to have the right amount of personal space... not too much and not too little.

You Be the Author

Rewrite *Personal Space Camp* and give it a new ending. Pretend Louis is a grown-up who never learned how to respect the personal space of others. What will happen to Louis? Will he have any friends? What kind of job will he have? In the box below, draw a picture of Louis as a grown-up.

_____

_____

_____

_____

_____

_____

_____

_____

_____

_____

_____

_____

_____

_____

_____

_____

More Than Words

Our author wants you to be her new illustrator.
In each box, draw a picture that goes with the words from the story *Personal Space Camp*.

My teacher used her cranky voice:
"Louis!" she said. "You are having problems with your personal space!"
"Why would she say that to me?" I thought. "I am a space expert!!!!!"

Suddenly, a light bulb went on in my head. Personal space wasn't what I thought it was at all!
"So that's why my teachers used their cranky voices," I thought to myself.

Time To Color